ANDY the ANCHOR

Written by

Kevin Cox

Illustrated by

Sasha Witter

HAPPY GOOD BOOKS

To my father in Heaven, my father on Earth, to my wife and daughter my true anchors of worth.

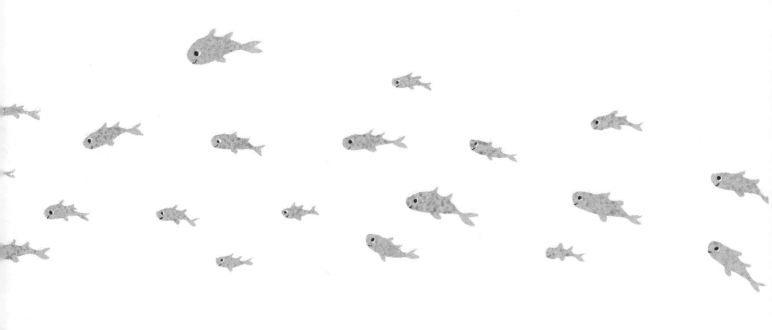

There once was an anchor
attached to a tanker
to help a good boat stay in place.

He was made of metal
and shaped so he could settle
with a rope attached to his face.

Why can't I be a steering wheel
or part of the keel
that makes the good boat go?

Why can't I be a rudder?
He started to mutter,
or an oar that moves to and fro?

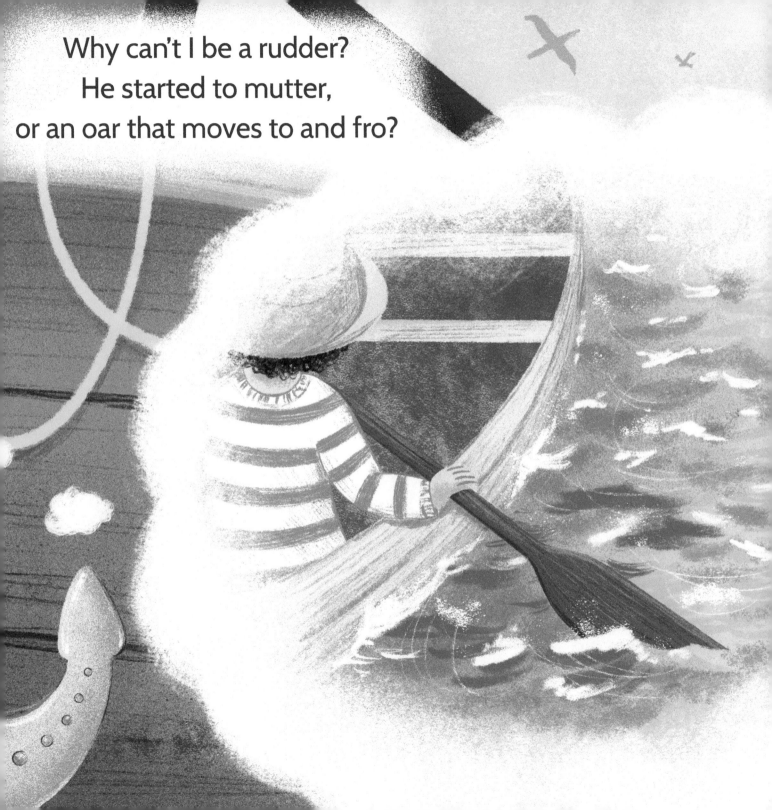

Then the sun went away,
and it started to rain.
Andy felt his first drop of water.

A hint of salt!
He began to exalt,
"Not bad for my first charter."

The good boat was shifting,
towards the rocks it was drifting.
For the ocean never gets tired.

On the waves they were tossed
without Andy all would be lost.
In stormy water, he felt inspired.

"I can't let this happen!"
He leapt from his captain
into the ocean so blue.

He felt a big whoosh
and started to swoosh.
He was doing what anchors do.

Curious fish soon arrived,
as he continued to dive,
to see his speedy descent.

They took up beside him
to help him and guide him
and deeper and deeper he went.

He met all sorts of creatures
with all sorts of features.
Even the plants waved, "Hi!"

But Andy kept sinking
as the ocean was thinking,
"Hey thanks for dropping by!"

Then all of a sudden
his gaze was flooded
by sand and shells galore.

He finally hit bottom.
The ocean floor caught him.
He never felt this feeling before!

The ocean rustled and tussled
applying its muscle,
but Andy didn't budge an inch.

He held to the rope
securing his boat.
That good ol' Andy didn't flinch.

He held like a boulder
digging in his shoulder
down into the depths below.

He realized his purpose
then stopped being nervous
and said, "Hey I was meant to lay low!"

And all through the night,
he nestled in tight
doing what anchors do best.

"Come high or low tide,
I'll be by your side -
always here so you can rest."

He realized: everything has a purpose.
Everything has a unique place,
and that put a giant smile on Andy's face!

THE
END!

CPSIA information can be obtained
at www.ICGtesting.com
Printed in the USA
LVHW072239080621
689763LV00017B/1188